I belong to
THE BEST BOOK CLUB EVER™
This is my book.

My name is

....

Will you please read it to me?

HAPPY BIRTHDAY OLIVER!

A Random House PICTUREBACK®

HAPPY BIRTHDAY OLIVER!

By Pierre Le-Tan

RANDOM HOUSE 🏠 NEW YORK

Library of Congress Cataloging in Publication Data: Le-Tan, Pierre. Happy birthday Oliver! SUMMARY: Excited about his birthday, Oliver is disappointed that no one seems to remember it. [1. Birthdays—Fiction. 2. Dogs—Fiction] I. Title. PZ7.L566Hap [E] 78-21762. ISBN: 0-394-83787-8 (B.C.); 0-394-83788-6 (trade); 0-394-93788-0 (lib. bdg.).

Manufactured in the United States of America.   C D E F G H I J   1 2 3 4 5 6 7 8 9 0

Oliver just couldn't go to sleep. Tomorrow would be his birthday, and what is more exciting than a birthday—except maybe Christmas?

Every year Mommy and Daddy did something special for Oliver's birthday. But this year they had not said a thing about it.

What if they had forgotten?

When Oliver finally fell asleep,
he dreamt about a wonderful birthday
party. All of his friends were there,
and they had brought presents for him.
Mommy had baked a big birthday
cake. And Daddy had bought balloons.

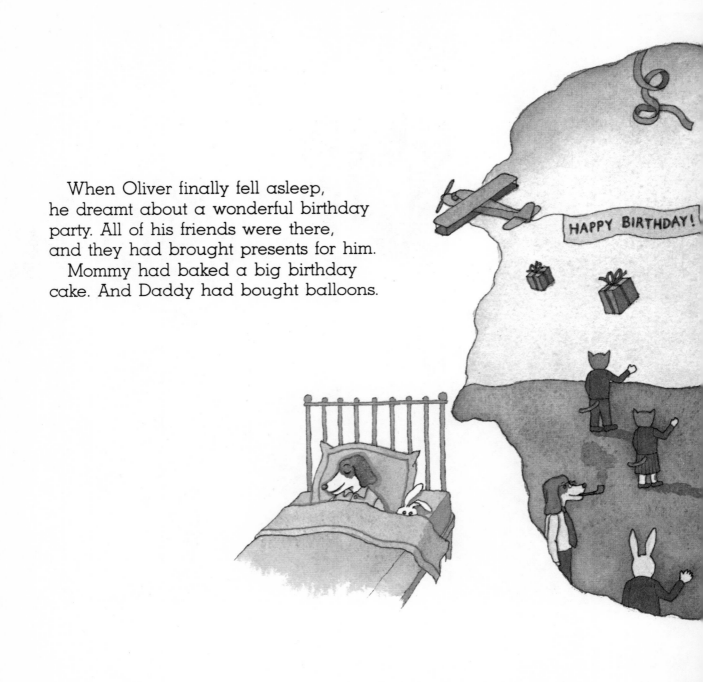

Next morning, when Oliver woke up, the house was quiet. He did not hear anyone wrapping presents. He did not smell a birthday cake baking in the oven. He *did* hear his father go down the stairs and off to work . . .

. . . just as he did on any ordinary day. Maybe I made a mistake, thought Oliver. Maybe today is not my birthday after all. Oliver looked at his calendar. He was right. Today was the day.

"Good morning, dear," said Oliver's mother when he
came into the kitchen for breakfast.
"Do you know what day it is today?" asked Oliver.

"Of course, Oliver," said his mother. "It's Friday."
Oliver was so disappointed he could not finish his
breakfast. They *have* forgotten my birthday! he thought.

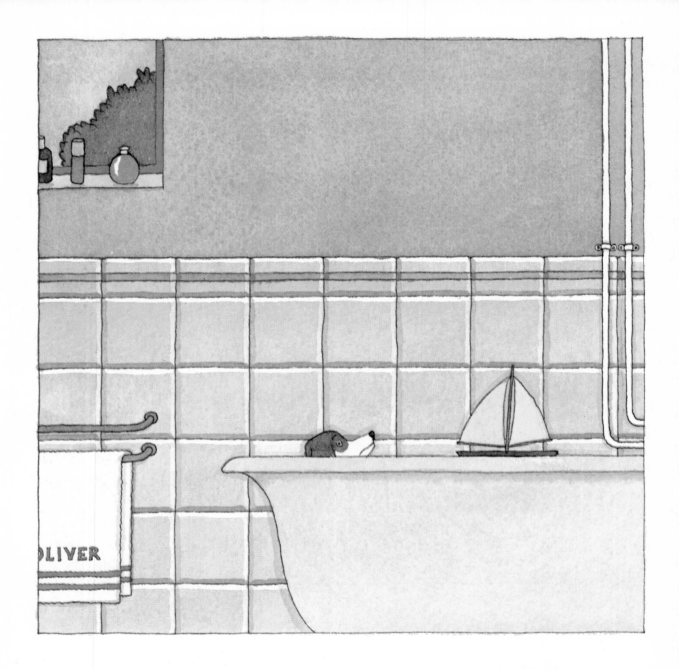

Maybe I am getting too big to have a *real* birthday,
thought Oliver as he took his bath.

He was so busy thinking about it that he forgot
to dry his ears.

On his way to school, Oliver did not look where
he was going. He was almost hit by a car.

"Watch where you're going!" shouted the driver.
Oliver did not even hear him.

That morning in class he could not answer a single
one of Miss Chestnut's questions.
Miss Chestnut asked him to stay after school.

When Oliver told her that his parents had forgotten his
birthday, she looked around for something to comfort him.
"Here you are," she said, handing Oliver a large feather.

All the way home, Oliver looked at Miss Chestnut's
feather. It would probably be his only birthday present.

"I think I will go straight to bed," said Oliver
as he stood outside the house.

But then the door opened. There stood Oliver's mother
in a long, pretty dress and a pointed hat.
"Happy Birthday, Oliver!" she said.

Oliver's father was dressed like a clown and the house
was decorated with balloons and streamers.
"Happy Birthday, Oliver!" said his father.

Oliver went to a corner of the living room. There he found heaps of birthday presents, all wrapped in brightly colored paper. He sat right down and began to open them.

There was a trumpet, a scrapbook with his name on it,
a model car, a ball, colored pens, a camel for his animal
collection, an airplane, a baseball cap, and red gloves.

Suddenly the doorbell rang. Oliver ran to open the door.

"*Happy Birthday, Oliver!*" cried all his friends.

Alexis had brought clown shoes for Oliver. Cousin Anna gave him a bottle of soap and a bubble blower. Ted brought funny little puppets, and Charles and Charlotte brought a baseball and bat.

"I'm lucky," thought Oliver as he sat on a chair, surrounded by his presents.

Soon all the children were laughing and playing.
It was a wonderful birthday party.

In a little while, Oliver's mother called the children to the table.

It was time for the birthday cake.

Daddy took a picture of Oliver blowing out all the candles.

Then each of them had a big piece of cake. Charles and Charlotte asked for two!

When the party was over, Oliver stood at the door
and waved good-by to his friends.
   "Happy Birthday, Oliver!" they called once more.

As he went up the stairs to bed, Oliver thanked
Mommy and Daddy for all the surprises. He looked
like the happiest boy in the world.

That night Oliver fell asleep without any trouble.
Good night, Oliver. Happy Birthday!